FIRE ENGINES

by Anne Rockwell

A Puffin Unicorn

PUFFIN UNICORN BOOKS

Published by the Penguin Group
Penguin Books USA Inc., 375 Hudson Street, New York, New York 10014, U.S.A.
Penguin Books Ltd, 27 Wrights Lane, London W8 5TZ, England
Penguin Books Australia Ltd, Ringwood, Victoria, Australia
Penguin Books Canada Ltd, 10 Alcorn Avenue, Toronto, Ontario, Canada M4V 3B2
Penguin Books (N.Z.) Ltd, 182-190 Wairau Road, Auckland 10, New Zealand
Penguin Books Ltd, Registered Offices: Harmondsworth, Middlesex, England

Library of Congress number 86-4464
ISBN 0-14-055250-2

Published in the United States by Dutton Children's Books,
a division of Penguin Books USA Inc.
Editor: Ann Durell
Designer: Isabel Warren-Lynch
Printed in Hong Kong by South China Printing Co.
First Puffin Unicorn Edition 1993
1 3 5 7 9 10 8 6 4 2

FIRE ENGINES is also available in hardcover
from Dutton Children's Books.

I like fire engines.

I like to watch the fire fighters

wash and polish their fire engines.

Ladder trucks have long ladders.

Motors raise the ladders high in the air.

Pumper trucks have hoses and pumps.

Water is pumped from a hydrant.

Hoses spray the water on fires.

Some fire engines have pumps

and hoses and ladders.

A firehouse ambulance comes
to help anyone who is hurt in a fire.

The fire chief drives a bright red car
and wears a white helmet and coat.

Some fire engines are yellow,

but I like red ones best.

Some fire engines are boats that
put out fires on ships and docks.

They spray water from the harbor.

Fire fighters are brave and strong.

Their fire engines are shiny and beautiful.

I want to be a fire fighter and drive
a real fire engine when I grow up.